FEELING LEFT OUT

First edition for the United States, Canada,
and the Philippines published 1991
by Barron's Educational Series, Inc.

Design David West Children's Book Design

All inquiries should be addressed to:
Barron's Educational Series, Inc.
250 Wireless Boulevard
Hauppauge, NY 11788

International Standard Book No. 0-8120-4658-7

Library of Congress Catalog Card No. 91-12113

Library of Congress Cataloging-in Publication Data

Petty, Kate.
    Feeling left out / Kate Petty and Charlotte Firmin. -- 1st ed.
        p.   cm. -- (Playgrounds)
    Summary: New to the neighborhood, Chris feels left out of various
games and social events.
    ISBN 0-8120-4658-7
    (1. Loneliness--Fiction.) I. Firmin, Charlotte. II. Title.
III. Series: Petty, Kate. Playgrounds.
PZ7.P44814Fe   1991
(E)--dc20   91-12113   CIP   AC

Printed in Belgium
1234   987654321

PLAYGROUNDS
FEELING LEFT OUT

Kate Petty and Charlotte Firmin

Barron's
New York • Toronto

Chris and his family live
next door to Lucy.
They haven't lived there long.

Lucy is glad to have someone
to play with. Games are
much more fun with two.

Chris walks to school with Lucy and
her mom. Lucy's mom says goodbye
to both of them at the playground gate.

Chris turns to talk to Lucy —
but Lucy isn't there. She's gone
to find the other girls.

In class, Miss Wood tells Chris
to sit with Joe. He's the best
soccer player in the school.

When it's time for gym, Chris hopes
that Joe will want him on his team.
But Joe chooses all of his old friends.

At playtime, when Chris tries to join in with the girls' game...

or the soccer game...

Nobody pays any attention to him.

Chris thinks up all sorts of ways to *make* them notice him.

"Go away, Chris."

"We don't want you."

Chris sits on a bench by himself.

He feels left out.

It's not a nice feeling.

Gina and Ahmet know how Chris is feeling.
"Do you want to play with us, Chris?"

"No, thanks." Chris would prefer
to be with Lucy or with Joe.

"Nobody wants to play with me,"
Chris tells his mom and dad.
"Sometimes I wish I was someone else —
a girl, like Lucy, or a good soccer
player, like Joe."

"But you're not someone else."
Chris's dad laughs. "You're you —
and we like you the way you are.
And so will everyone else —
just give them time."

Chris doesn't like being alone for long.
He joins Gina and Ahmet's game.

They are happy to play with him.

So, Chris still plays with Lucy at home,

and he sits next to Joe in class,

and he plays with Gina and Ahmet
during recess. That's all right.

Chris doesn't try to make people
notice him anymore –
but they notice him anyway.
Lucy wants him to be
her dancing partner.

So does Gina.

Joe wants him to be on his quiz team.

So does Ahmet.

It's nice to be wanted.

There are still times when
Chris feels left out.
Lucy has an all-girls birthday party.

Joe has a soccer party.

So when it is Chris's turn,
he has a *huge* birthday party,
with lots of games and balloons.

His mom and dad say he can invite everyone, because he doesn't want anyone to feel left out.

THINGS TO DO...

Draw a picture of Chris in the playground.
Or draw a picture of yourself in the playground.

Talk about why Chris didn't have anyone to
play with at school.
Or talk about how Chris felt when no one wanted
to play with him.
Or talk about a time when you felt left out.

Make a play or use puppets to tell the
story in the book.
Or make up a play about a time when somebody
in your class was left out.

Remember that everybody feels left out
sometimes, especially in a new group
of people. Groups can change all the time.
You don't have to be with the same friend or
friends all the time. You can be friends with
lots of different people at different times.
Be friendly with everyone – especially those
you think might be feeling left out themselves.

PRINTED IN BELGIUM BY

proost

INTERNATIONAL BOOK PRODUCTION